Welcome to
Whisker Haven

By Brittany Rubiano
Illustrated by the Disney Storybook Art Team

A GOLDEN BOOK • NEW YORK

One day, Ariel's kitten, Treasure, was playing with her toy boat on the beach outside the palace. Suddenly, a glowing ball of light floated up to her.

It grew larger and larger, until . . .

. . . it turned into a
glittering hummingbird!

Splash!

Treasure was so surprised
that she fell into the water.

The hummingbird fluttered her wings,
then took off toward Ariel's palace. Curious,
Treasure decided to follow.

The little bird went into the palace and
down a long hallway.

Where is she going? thought Treasure.

Finally, the hummingbird stopped in front of a large doorway. She clapped her wings, and a beautiful castle appeared. Treasure followed her toward it.

Whoosh! She fell through a maze of glittering lights . . .

. . . and landed on a cool, tile floor.

"Shimmering seashells!"

she whispered. She was in another palace—
no, it was a *Pawlace*—and it was glorious.

"Welcome to Whisker Haven," said the hummingbird. "I'm Ms. Featherbon, and I need your help."

Just then, a pony came running over.
"I'm so happy you're here!" she cried.

"Pumpkin's in trouble.
Follow me!"

"Who are you?" asked Treasure.

"Who's Pumpkin?"

But there was no time for introductions.

The pony led Treasure and Ms. Featherbon to a balcony.

"cartwheeling catfish!" Treasure exclaimed when she peered over the edge. "What happened?"

Below, the Pawlace was filled with water.
A fluffy white dog was floating on her bed.
"Pumpkin left her bathtub running, and
it overflowed," explained the pony.

"Petite!" Pumpkin called up
to the pony. "Help me!"

Petite looked at Treasure. "I can't swim," she said. "And my feathers aren't flippers," Ms. Featherbon added. "That's why we need you!"

Treasure smiled. "I love the water!" she said, then dove into the rising waves.

She was determined to get the water out of the Pawlace!

Water was quickly filling the Pawlace. Pumpkin jumped onto a flagpole and held on tight!

Treasure swam to the front doors of the Pawlace. She pulled as hard as she could, but the doors wouldn't open.

The kitten swam and swam, looking for something that might help. She passed a drifting bed, a lamp, and a leash.

A leash—that was it! Treasure gathered all the leashes she could find and tied them together to make one long rope. Then she swam to the surface and threw the leash rope up to the balcony.
"Petite! Catch!"

Petite caught the leash with her teeth.
Ms. Featherbon helped.

Treasure dove underwater again.

She tied the other end of the leash rope to one of the door handles. She and her friends pulled and pulled, until . . .

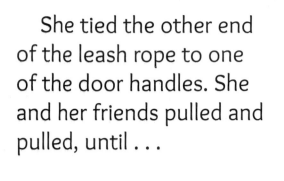

Whoosh!

The door opened, and water began to drain out of the Pawlace.

Petite and Ms. Featherbon cheered with delight. Treasure floated up to them in a large, shiny bubble from Pumpkin's bath. Ms. Featherbon popped it with her beak.

"Thanks for bursting my bubble!" said Treasure.

"Thank you, Treasure!" exclaimed Pumpkin from the soggy Pawlace floor. "I have to get back to Cinderella's castle now."

"Not so fast, messy missy!" said Ms. Featherbon. "You have some cleaning to do."

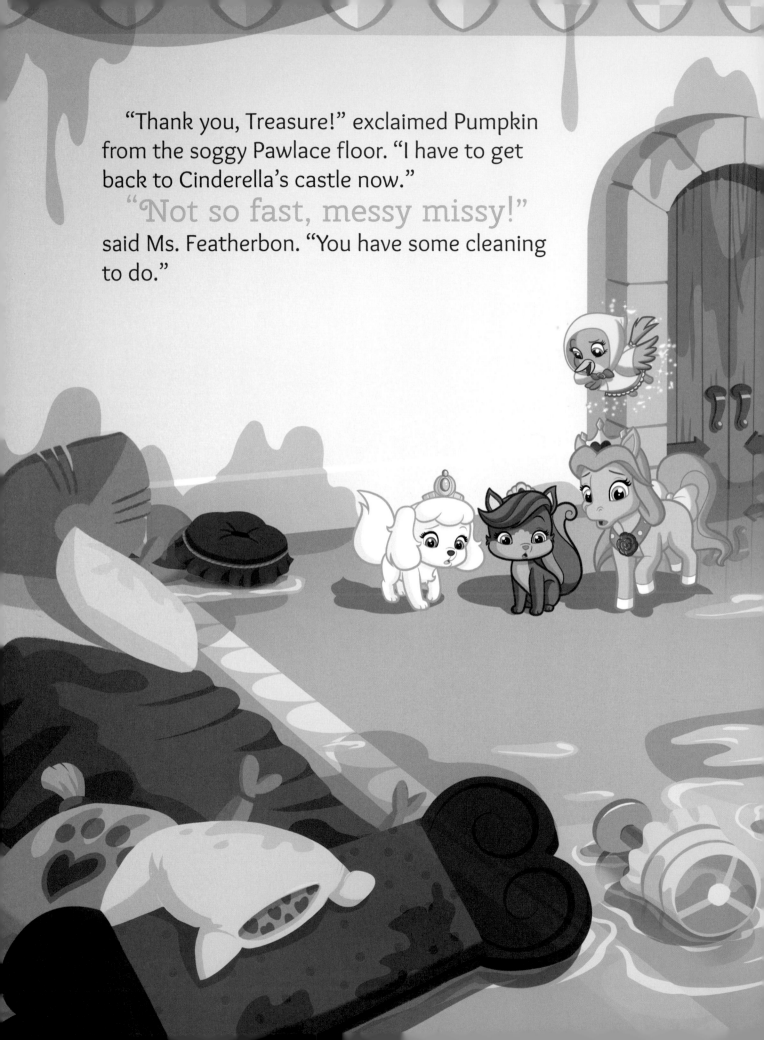

Treasure and Petite offered to help, and together the new friends mopped up the water,

singing and dancing the whole time.

Soon the Pawlace was positively sparkling!

Pumpkin thanked Treasure, Petite, and Ms. Featherbon.
"Hearts, hooves, paws!" cheered the four friends.
They couldn't wait for their next adventure together!